David Copperfield

Charles Dickens

Adapted by Richard Widdows

GALLERY BOOKS
An Imprint of W. H. Smith Publishers Inc.
112 Madison Avenue
New York City 10016

This book was devised and produced by
Multimedia Publications (UK) Ltd.

Editor: Richard Widdows (Acorn Press)
Designer: Janette Place
Production: Arnon Orbach

First published in the United States of America 1985 by
Gallery Books, an imprint of W. H. Smith Publishers Inc.,
112 Madison Avenue, New York, NY 10016

ISBN 0 8317 2107 3

Typeset by Waveney Typesetters, Norwich, Norfolk
Origination by Clifton Studios Ltd., London
Printed in Italy by Amilcare Pizzi SpA., Milan

Contents

The Life of Charles Dickens

Charles John Huffham Dickens was born on 7 February 1812, in the English coastal town of Portsmouth, where his father, John Dickens, was a clerk in the Navy Pay Office. John Dickens was 26 when Charles was born and was an excitable, extravagant man who liked to entertain in style — a style that his meagre salary as a clerk was unable to support. This was to lead him into a succession of financial crises throughout his life.

The second of eight children, Charles was a delicate, sensitive child, unable to join in the play of other children, and he withdrew into books. Later in life, recalling his boyhood days, he wrote: "When I think of it, the picture always arises in my mind of a summer evening, the boys at play in the churchyard and I sitting on my bed, reading as if for life."

The books that he read, introduced to him by his father — books such as *Robinson Crusoe*, *The Arabian Nights*, *Don Quixote* and a child's *Tom Jones* — created for him a world of magic, wonder and adventure, a world that he himself was so vividly to create for others to enjoy in his own books.

At the age of 12 the childhood of Dickens came to a sudden and dramatic end. His father, unable to pay his large debts, was packed off to the Marshalsea Debtors' Prison in London. Within a few days the rest of the family were to join him there — all, that is, except Charles, whose education was cut short and who was made to earn his living, washing bottles, at Warren's Blacking Factory. This experience proved so shocking and humiliating to the boy that it was to haunt him for the rest of his life. "No words can express the secret agony of my soul . . . I felt my early hopes of growing up to be a learned and distinguished man crushed in my breast."

Though soon re-united with his family, the previous easy life enjoyed by Charles was never to return. Two years later, at the age of 14, his irregular and inadequate schooling ended and he began work as a clerk in a lawyer's office in Gray's Inn, London. This experience, again not a happy one, gave him two things — a lifelong loathing of the legal profession and much raw material for many of his later novels.

Dickens then became a reporter on the parliamentary newspaper *True Sun*, where his natural talent for reporting and keen observation was first recognized. He taught himself shorthand and, on the *Mirror of Parliament*, and then the *Morning Chronicle*, he was soon acknowledged as the best parliamentary reporter of the age.

In 1833, now very much the young man about town, Dickens wrote his first piece of fiction: *A Dinner at Poplar Walk*, in the *Old Monthly Magazine*. Asked by the editor to contribute more, under the pen name 'Boz', Dickens wrote a series of pieces that were collected and published in 1836 under the title *Sketches by Boz*.

The modest success of *Sketches* was followed by the enormously popular and successful *Pickwick Papers*, which was published in monthly instalments in 1836 and 1837. Pickwick became a national hero overnight, and his exploits were followed by an average of 40,000 readers. Though not yet 30, Dickens was now rich and famous.

Two days after the publication of Pickwick, Dickens married Catherine Hogarth, daughter of a fellow journalist. "So perfect a creature never breathed," he wrote of her at the time, "she had not a fault." But with time his view of her was to change, and in later years he was to admit, "She is amiable and complying but nothing on earth would make her understand me." They were to separate in 1858, when Dickens was 46.

Throughout his life Dickens enjoyed travelling. In the 1840s he journeyed to Scotland, America, France, Switzerland and Italy. And throughout this period he poured out a succession of novels that exposed the cruelty, hypocrisy and appalling poverty of early Victorian society, novels such as *Oliver Twist*, *Nicholas Nickleby*, *The Old Curiosity Shop*, *Barnaby Rudge*, *A Christmas Carol*, *Martin Chuzzlewit*, and *Dombey and Son*.

Even his novel writing (which continued to be published in monthly instalments) proved inadequate for his boundless energy and restless spirit. In the 1840s, apart from all his major novels, and work on *David Copperfield* (published in 1850), he started a daily newspaper, the *Daily News*, and a weekly magazine, *Household Words*, in addition to writing a travel book *American Notes* and a three-volume *Child's History of England*.

In all that he wrote Dickens strove to draw people together and lead them to a better understanding of each other. As he himself believed, "In this world a great deal of bitterness among us arises from an imperfect understanding of one another."

But as he grew older, the subjects he wrote of grew bleaker and the mood more grim. *Bleak House, Hard Times, Little Dorrit, A Tale of Two Cities, Great Expectations, Our Mutual Friend* and his unfinished novel, *The Mystery of Edwin Drood*, all reflect a growing pessimism.

Despite a steady decline in health, Dickens continued to give dramatic public readings of his works to packed houses in both Britain and the United States, which he visited again in 1867–68. Of these a contemporary witness reported, "He seemed to be physically transformed as he passed from one character to another; he had as many distinct voices as his books had characters; he held at command the fountains of laughter and tears . . . When he sat down it was not mere applause that followed, but a passionate outburst of love for the man."

But the strain proved too much and on 8 June 1870, during a farewell series of talks in England, he suffered a stroke, and the next day he died at his home, Gad's Hill Place, near Rochester, Kent, at the age of 58.

Two days after his death Queen Victoria wrote in her diary, "He is a very great loss. He had a large loving mind and the strongest sympathy with the poorer classes." On 14 June he was buried in Poet's Corner, Westminster Abbey, close to the monuments of Chaucer and Shakespeare.

Charles Dickens in his study at Gad's Hill Place, his home near Rochester, Kent, reproduced by kind permission of the Trustees of the Dickens House (*Dickens' Dream* by R. W. Buss)

Introduction

IN the preface to the 1869 edition of *David Copperfield*, published just before his death, Dickens wrote: "Of all my books, I like this the best. It will be easily believed that I am a fond parent to every child of my fancy, and that no-one can ever love that family as dearly as I love them. But, like many fond parents, I have in my heart of hearts a favourite child. And his name is *David Copperfield*."

Dickens started the book in London in February 1849 and finished it at Broadstairs, on the Kent coast, in October 1850. Like most of his novels it was published as a "part-work", monthly instalments of 32 pages with two engraved illustrations.

Parts of *David Copperfield* clearly reflect parts of Dickens' own life. In fact he originally intended to write his life story and publish it after his death, but he soon abandoned the idea and put many of his experiences and feelings into the novel instead.

John Dickens, his father, is the obvious inspiration for Mr Micawber; he had all Mr Micawber's virtues — charm, generosity, eloquence, optimism — and the same hopeless irresponsibility with money. When his father was sent to prison for debt the 12-year-old Charles went to work at a "blacking" (ink) factory near the River Thames, a business managed by a friend of the Dickens family. He earned six shillings (the cost of an ice-cream in today's money) for 68 hours' work a week. Though he was earning money badly needed by his family, Charles felt humiliated and abandoned.

Many other events in Dickens' life are present in *David Copperfield*. David's miserable time at Salem House school is an echo of Dickens' short attendance at Wellington House Academy, the school his father sent him to after his job at the factory, and Mr Creakle is accurately based on Dickens' own headmaster, William Jones. Like Dickens, David begins his literary career as a reporter and writer of short stories, and soon becomes a famous novelist; like Dickens, he produces a houseful of children whom he adores.

Why is *David Copperfield* still read with such delight today? First of all, it is simply a great story — romantic, but also realistic and believable. Second, it excites all our emotions, from rib-tickling laughter to tears of pity. Third, it is almost impossible not to like David, to feel for him and wish him well. Most of his qualities — modesty, frankness, trustworthiness, honesty, goodwill — are ones we admire, and his frailties are understandable and endearing. And last, of course, it contains a cast of wonderful, larger-than-life characters: Peggotty, Mr Micawber, Uriah Heep, Betsey Trotwood, and a host of others. Their names will last as long as Dickens' own.

1 Early Days

To begin my story with the beginning of my life, I record that I was born (or so I have been informed and believe) on a Friday in March, at twelve o'clock at night. This event took place at my mother's house near the village of Blunderstone, in the county of Suffolk.

My father's eyes had been closed on the light of this world six months when mine opened on it — a fact which helps to account for the sudden appearance of a strange visitor on the very day of my own arrival.

This bold lady, having first startled my poor mother by looking in at the window, then entered the house and approached her as she sat by the fire.

"Mrs David Copperfield, I think?" she asked.

"Yes," replied my mother, faintly.

"You have heard, I dare say, of Miss Betsey Trotwood, aunt of your late husband? Well, now you see her!"

Before she could muster a word in reply, my mother burst into tears.

"Oh come, come! Don't do that!" said Miss Trotwood, giving her a handkerchief. "Why bless my heart, look at you — you're only a child, and here you are with child yourself. Now, what's the matter, my dear?"

"I'm — I'm all in a tremble. I don't know what will happen. I'll die, I'm sure I'll die!"

"That, my child, is absolute nonsense! What you need is a good strong cup of tea. Now, what do you call your girl?"

"I don't know that it will be a girl."

"No, no. I don't mean the baby. I mean what do you call your servant girl?"

"Oh! Peggotty."

"Peggotty! How very extraordinary!"

"Her Christian name is Clara," explained my mother patiently. "But that's the same as mine, so I call her by her surname to avoid confusion."

"I see," said Miss Trotwood, walking to the door. "Peggotty! We need some tea! Don't dawdle now!"

She resumed her seat by the fire, still wearing her bonnet. "I have no doubt that this baby of yours will be a girl," she continued. "Now, from the moment of the birth this girl —"

"Perhaps boy."

"Don't contradict me, child! I intend to be your daughter's godmother, and I beg you to call her Betsey Trotwood Copperfield. There will be no mistakes in life with *this* Betsey Trotwood. There must be no trifling with *her* affections, poor dear. *She* must be well brought up and well guarded. And I must make that my care!"

Before my mother could contest this suggestion she collapsed in her chair, just as Peggotty came in with a tray. "It's the doctor you need, ma'am," she said firmly, "not a cup of tea!"

"Well don't just stand there, Peggotty!" cried Miss Trotwood. "Be off and fetch the man. Quickly!"

While all around her busied themselves with carrying my mother upstairs and preparing for the great happening, Miss Trotwood stopped up her ears with cotton-wool and sat down by the fire, with her embroidery as company. And she was still there several hours later when Peggotty entered the room carrying the new-born child in her ample arms.

"Would you like to see the baby, Miss Trotwood? He's a strong little thing, with a pair of lungs like the wind at sea."

The visitor rose from her chair. "How is she?"

"Oh, she's comfortable, ma'am. The doctor says she's as comfortable as a young mother can expect to be under these melancholy domestic circumstances."

"Peggotty, you would appear to have a mind every bit as wondrous as your name. I meant the baby. How is she?"

"My name seems no less wondrous than your understandin', ma'am. The baby is a boy. We've called him David, after his father — David Copperfield."

I am told that my great aunt said not a word,

but picked up her basket, put on her coat and walked out into the night. She vanished like a discontented fairy — and never returned.

Looking back into my infancy, the first objects I can remember as standing out by themselves from a confusion of things are my mother, with her pretty hair and youthful shape, and Peggotty, with hardly any shape at all. I remember, too, that we were both a little afraid of Peggotty, and submitted ourselves in most matters to her direction. And I remember that I was very happy.

Late one summer evening, when I was eight or so, I was gazing out of the window on to the garden when I saw my mother bidding goodbye

to a tall, dark gentleman. His name was Mr Murdstone, and he had walked home with us from church on several Sundays. When my mother came into the room, she looked even more beautiful than usual.

"I hope you had a pleasant evenin', ma'am," inquired Peggotty, rather coolly.

"Oh yes, thank you, Peggotty," replied my mother, taking off her bonnet in front of the mirror. "I had a very pleasant evening indeed!"

"A stranger or so makes an agreeable change," suggested Peggotty.

"You don't approve of my going out, do you, Peggotty? But tell me, what should I do? Shave my head and hide my face, or disfigure myself with a burn?"

"Mr Copperfield wouldn't have liked such a one as this. That I say and that I swear."

"Oh stop, Peggotty! Stop!" cried my mother, bursting into tears. "You'll upset David!"

There was an awkward silence during which everyone regretted what had been said.

"Perhaps what he needs is a holiday by the sea," said Peggotty finally. "Would you like to go along and stay with my brother and his family at Yarmouth, Davy?"

"Is your brother an agreeable man?" I asked.

"Oh, what an agreeable man he is!" cried Peggotty, holding up her hands. "Then there's the sea and the boats and the beach and my nephew Ham and little Em'ly —"

"I'd love to go," I said, and the arrangement was sealed with hugs and kisses.

The day soon arrived for our trip to Yarmouth, which would be by horse and cart. The carrier, whose name was Barkis — a man of remarkable few words — owned what must have been the slowest horse in the world, so the journey took most of the day, and we were thankful for Peggotty's fine pies.

When we eventually arrived on the edge of Yarmouth we were met by Peggotty's nephew. "There's my Ham," she cried, "growed out of all knowin'."

Peggotty was right, for this 'boy' she had described to me was now a huge strong fellow of six feet, and broad in proportion. He took our bags and put me on his back to guide us along the beach.

Suddenly he stopped. "Yon's our house, Mas'r Davy!" he said, putting me down.

I looked in all directions, as far as I could see, but I could make out no house. There was an upturned boat not far away, high and dry off the ground, with a smoking iron funnel for a chimney; but nothing else in the way of habitation was visible to me. "That's it?" I asked. "That ship-looking thing?" They both said it was, and I could not have been more charmed by the idea of living in it had it been Aladdin's palace.

From this unusual home appeared a bearded, pipe-smoking fisherman and, behind him at the door, a girl not much older than myself.

"Davy, this is my brother," said Peggotty, "and that there's little Em'ly."

"We're glad to see you, sir," said Mr Peggotty with a broad smile. "You'll find us rough but you'll find us ready. And I hope you'll stay as long as you've a mind to."

The girl darted into the house. "She's a shy one, that little Em'ly," laughed Mr Peggotty. "God bless her. Now come on, young Davy, I'll show you your room."

After tea, when the door was shut and all was made snug, this place seemed to me the most enchanting retreat the imagination could conceive. Emily had overcome her shyness and sat next to me by the fire; later, when Peggotty tucked me up in bed, she told me that Emily was an orphan whom Mr Peggotty had adopted as his very own — as he had done with Ham.

The next morning I was up early and soon out on the beach with Emily, picking up stones.

"You're quite a sailor, I expect?" I said.

"No," replied Emily. "I'm afraid of the sea."

"Afraid!" I said, looking out across the water. "I'm not!"

"But it's cruel. It's very cruel, the sea. I've seen it tear a boat as big as our house to pieces."

"I hope it wasn't the boat that —"

"That my father was drownded in? No, not that one. I never see that boat."

"Nor him?"

Emily shook her pretty head. "Not to remember, anyhow."

"I never saw my father, either."

"Your father was a gentleman — mine was a fisherman. And so's my uncle."

"He seems a very good man, Mr Peggotty."

"Good? If I was ever to be a lady I'd give him a sky-blue coat with diamond buttons and a pipe made out of silver."

"You'd like to be a lady, then?"

"Oh yes. I'd like it more than anything."

We walked a long way and loaded ourselves up with all kinds of curious things before turning back towards Mr Peggotty's home. "Look at you two," he said as we went in for breakfast. "Just like a pair of young thrushes!"

The blissful days at Yarmouth flew by and soon Mr Barkis, who lived not far away, arrived with his cart and trusty steed. It broke my heart to leave Emily, but Mr Peggotty said I would be welcome at any time — and Peggotty assured me as we set off for Blunderstone that her brother was a man of his word.

After that, however, she went strangely silent, and as we neared our village I saw a tear or two trickle down her plump cheek.

"Why, Peggotty, what is it?"

"Wait, Davy — wait till we get inside."

Peggotty took me into the kitchen and closed the door behind us.

"What is it, Peggotty? What's the matter?"

"I should have told you afore now," she said quietly, holding my hand, "but, well, you were so busy and so happy I couldn't exactly bring my mind to it. Now what do you think, Davy — you've got a father! Come and see him."

"I don't want to see him!"

"And your mother?" said Peggotty.

My heart was pounding. She led me into the parlour and went back to the kitchen. On one side of the fire sat my mother; on the other stood Mr Murdstone. My mother got up to come to me, but suddenly stopped.

"Now Clara, control yourself!" snapped Mr Murdstone. "Always control yourself!"

He walked towards me and held out his hand. "Davy boy, how do you do?"

I shook his hand but could say nothing. I went and kissed my mother, but I could not look at her — and I could not look at him.

I left the room and ran into the kitchen. "Oh, Peggotty, I don't like him. I don't want a father, especially not Mr Murdstone!"

"I knew it would be hard for you, Davy. That's why I took you to the seaside. It's going to be hard for me too, but we'll just have to make the best of it, won't we?"

"Is he here to stay?" I asked, already knowing the dreadful answer.

"Yes, Davy, he is — and his sister arrives tomorrow evening!"

I crept upstairs and found that my dear bedroom, like everything in the house, had been changed. My mother came up to see me in my new room, but Mr Murdstone soon followed and sent her down, telling her that she must compose herself and be firm with me from then on.

2 I Am Sent to School

I could see that Mr Murdstone was fond of my mother, but I'm afraid I liked him none the better for that. I longed for a word of encouragement or even explanation, of welcome home, of reassurance that it *was* home. It may at least have made me respect him rather than just hate him.

The following evening his sister arrived, and Peggotty led me into the hall to meet her. A miserable looking lady she was, dark and unsmiling like her brother, and as far as I could make out she had come to stay for good; indeed within hours she was running the entire household.

As the days passed, a suffocating gloom settled on our house, with never a smile to brighten any day, and with Sundays even more of a trial than the rest. My only consolation were the storybooks left by my father, and I spent hour after hour buried in *Robinson Crusoe, The Arabian Nights* and many other tales of adventure in my room.

Firmness was the one virtue on which both Mr and Miss Murdstone insisted. An iron discipline reigned, with my mother as much a subject as myself. There was occasional talk about my going to boarding-school, but in the meantime I continued my lessons at home.

I was scrutinized by all three adults during these lessons, and they were the greatest burden of my dreary life. The influence of the Murdstones was like the cruel fascination of two snakes on a wretched bird.

One evening Mr Murdstone held in his hand a cane, which he now and again swished to impress me.

"Now, David," he said, putting the cane on the table, "you must be far more careful today than usual with your answers."

I was indeed extremely careful, but I still faltered several times. Suddenly Mr Murdstone stood up. "You must and *will* learn your lessons off by heart, boy. Do you understand?"

"But Mr Murdstone, sir! I find it difficult to do my work with you and Miss Murdstone so close by me."

"I will not tolerate such impudence, boy!" he shouted, flexing the cane with his hands. "You and I will go upstairs!"

"Please, Edward. No!" pleaded my mother.

"Are you a *perfect* fool, Clara," interrupted Miss Murdstone. "You are too soft with the boy. He needs discipline — and discipline he shall have!"

Mr Murdstone walked me up to my room slowly and gravely, like an executioner leading his doomed prisoner, and once there gripped my head under his arm. But I wriggled free for a moment, pleading with him not to beat me.

It was only a moment, for he then grabbed my

collar and cut me heavily with the cane, and in the same instant I clenched the hand that held me between my teeth, and bit it through. Even now, it sets my teeth on edge to think of it.

He beat me then, as though he would have beaten me to death. But above all our noise I still heard the running on the stairs — my mother crying out — and Peggotty. Then he was gone, and the door locked. And I was lying, hot and sore and torn, on the floor.

When I became quiet I lay listening for a while, but there was not a sound. My cuts were sore and stiff, and made me ache if I tried to move, but they were nothing to the guilt I felt.

Miss Murdstone appeared next morning before I was out of bed and told me I was free to walk in the garden for half an hour, and no longer. I did so, with some difficulty that first day, and did so every morning of my imprisonment, which lasted five days; and I saw no-one except that awesome creature during that time.

The length of those five tormented days I cannot convey to anyone; they occupy the place of years in my memory. Every detail of that room, every sound that reached me from the world outside it, are etched on my mind.

On the last evening of my punishment, I suddenly heard my own name, spoken in a whisper on the other side of the door.

"Is that you, Peggotty?"

"Yes, my own precious Davy. But be as soft as a mouse, or the cat will hear us!"

"How's mama, Peggotty? Is she angry with me?"

"No, not very."

"What's going to be done with me?"

"School, Davy. Near London. Tomorrow."

"Shall I see mama?"

"Yes, in the mornin'. 'Night, darlin' boy."

"Goodnight, Peggotty — and thank you!"

In the morning, at breakfast, I ran into my mother's arms and begged her to forgive me.

"Oh, Davy!" she said. "That you could hurt anyone I love! Try to be better, pray to be better. I forgive you, but I'm so grieved that you should have such bad passions in your heart."

Mr Barkis was to take me to Yarmouth, where next day I would board the coach to London. There, at the ticket office, I would be met by a master and escorted to the school, which was across the river in the district of Blackheath.

My mother came out to see me off on a fine summer's day, with Miss Murdstone hovering by her side. "Goodbye, my child," she said softly. "You are going for your own good. You will come home in the holidays and be a better boy. God bless you, my darling!"

The lazy horse had gone about half a mile — and I had almost stopped crying — when Mr Barkis suddenly pulled him up as Peggotty dashed out from a hedge.

"Here, Davy," she said, handing me a paper bag. "I've baked some cakes for your journey — and here's a purse with seven shillings in it. From your mother, with her love." And with that she feel into deep sobs and turned to walk quickly back to the house.

After some miles I took out Peggotty's bag and offered Mr Barkis one of her cakes, which he consumed in one gulp.

"Did she make that?" he inquired.

I told him that Peggotty did all our cooking.

"Do she though!" said Mr Barkis, stirring in his seat and turning his gaze on me. "No sweethearts, I believe? No person walks with her?"

I said I didn't think that Peggotty had ever had a sweetheart.

"Didn't she, though!" said Mr Barkis. "Well, I'll tell you what. If you was writin' to her, p'raps you'd recollect to say that Barkis is willin'."

"That Barkis is willing," I repeated. "Is that all the message?"

"Aye, that's all. You just tell her that. Barkis is willin'."

On my arrival at Salem House, for that was the name of my school, I was sent to wait outside the study of the headmaster, one Mr Creakle. The place was almost deserted, and I could not help but wonder, as I sat trying to read my book, why I could neither see nor hear any other boys.

The door opened and there stood before me a stout, bald man whose fiery eyes seemed to be sunk deep in his head. He pointed for me to enter, then banged the door shut behind him.

"So you're Copperfield, eh?"

"Yes, sir," I replied, quite quaking with fear.

"I have the pleasure of knowing your step-father," said Mr Creakle, taking me by the ear, "and a worthy man he is. I know him and he knows me. Do you know me, boy, eh?"

"Not yet, sir," I said, flinching with pain.

"Not yet. But you soon will, eh?"

"I hope so, sir."

"You're very smart, Copperfield, very smart," said Mr Creakle, finally letting go of my ear, "for a boy who bites!" He took a sheet of card from his desk and held it up before me:

"What does this say, boy, eh?"

"It says 'I bite', sir."

"You'll wear this on your back, boy, until I say that you can take it off!"

"Oh, please, sir, must I?"

Mr Creakle raised his cane above his head. "When I say I'll do a thing, boy, I do it," he shouted, bringing the cane crashing down on the desk, "and when I say I'll have a thing done, I will have it done! Turn around, boy!"

He fixed the card to my jacket and ordered me out of his study.

It transpired that the other boys were not due back for the half-year term until the next day. I was dreading their making fun of me, so it was a happy circumstance for me that it was Tommy Traddles, a plump, friendly character, who was the first to return. He found it very amusing, and used the card as a form of introduction to the others with the words, "Look here, here's a game!" Some boys mocked me, saying "Lie down, sir!" and calling me dogs' names, but on the whole it was better than I had expected.

Traddles' last introduction was to J. Steerforth. I was taken before this boy, who was said to be a great scholar and athlete, and was at least half-a-dozen years my senior, as if before a magistrate.

"What money have you got, Copperfield?"

I told him seven shillings.

"You had better give it to me to take care of," he said. "At least, you can if you like. You needn't if you don't want to."

I opened my purse into his hand.

"Do you want to spend anything now?"

"No thank you, sir."

"Perhaps you'd like to spend a shilling or so on a bottle of redcurrant wine for later, up in the dormitory," suggested Steerforth. "You belong to my dormitory, I believe."

I said yes, I should like that.

"Good. I dare say you'll be glad to spend another shilling or so on almond cake, and another shilling or so on biscuits, and another on fruit, eh?"

I said I would like that, too.

"I can go out when I like," said Steerforth, "so I'll smuggle the stuff in for you." And with that he pocketed the seven coins and walked away.

I was a little worried, I confess, about handing over my mother's present so readily, but Traddles took me by the arm. "Don't worry, Copperfield," he said quietly. "Steerforth's not a bully. You'll see."

Indeed I did, for that evening when we went to bed there was a whole seven shillings' worth laid out on my bed.

"There you are, young Copperfield, and a right royal spread you've got."

We did the feast proud, and continued talking in whispered tones until well past the time to go to sleep.

"Goodnight, young Copperfield," said Steerforth. "I'll take good care of you."

"You're very kind," I replied. "Goodnight."

It was Steerforth's clever ploy that, after a few days, had my card removed. He informed Mr Creakle that it was a nuisance when masters wished to hit me with their canes as they passed,

and it was then taken off, to my great relief.

There was only one event in this half-year, outside the daily life of the school, which still survives in my mind: a visit — my only one — of some dear acquaintances. I was called out from

the class one late summer afternoon and there, in the courtyard, stood Mr Peggotty and Ham.

I could not stop myself bursting into tears at the sight of them, and felt a little ashamed.

"Cheer up, Mas'r Davy!" said Ham. "Why, how you've growed!"

"Ain't he growed!" echoed Mr Peggotty.

"We brought you some victuals, Mas'r Davy," said Ham, bending over a fisherman's basket; and he produced a lobster, crabs and a great bag of shrimps.

"They're all boiled ready," explained Mr Peggotty. "We was bringin' down a lug to Gravesend so we thought we'd take the liberty of comin' over to pay a visit."

"Oh, I'm so glad you did, and thank you. Tell me, Mr Peggotty, how's dear Emily?"

"She's uncommon well, Davy," he replied, "uncommon well. And she's getting to be somethin' of a woman, now."

Ham beamed with delight at the very mention of her name. "Her learnin', too, Mas'r Davy."

"And writin'!" added Mr Peggotty. "So large it is, you might see it anywheres."

I was telling them about the school — and trying to conceal its unpleasant aspects — when Steerforth walked across the courtyard towards us, carrying a cricket bat.

"What are you doing out here, young Copperfield?" he asked.

"Steerforth, these are two Yarmouth boatmen who are relations of my nurse, Peggotty. They've come over from Gravesend to see me."

Steerforth was charming and amusing — he had an ability to put anyone at their ease in a moment that I have not yet seen rivalled by any person — and by the time of his departure a few minutes later was being invited up to Yarmouth to view their strange home and go sailing with Mr Peggotty upon the sea.

3 Tragedy and Neglect

Apart from the delight I gave to the whole dormitory by telling the stories I had learned from my books, I remember little of what happened at school in my second term until my birthday — an anniversary that turned out to be the most memorable of my life.

After breakfast I was told I had a visitor and there, in the courtyard, stood Peggotty.

"Peggotty!" I cried. "What a lovely surprise!"

"I wish it were, Davy," she replied solemnly, "I only wish it were. But I'm afraid I've got bad news for you."

"Mama — is she all right?"

"No, Davy, she's not. Your mother has passed on."

"Mother, dead? Oh no, no!"

"There, there, my darlin' boy. She was always a frail creature, never very strong. And now she's gone."

"What — what will become of me, Peggotty?"

"First, you'll come home with me for the funeral, Davy. Then it'll be up to Mr Murdstone to decide what's to be done for the best."

I burst into uncontrollable sobs — whether at the death of my mother or the prospect of the Murdstones in sole control of me, I cannot say.

"There now, Davy," said Peggotty, holding me close to her. "We must both be very brave."

Mr Murdstone took no heed of me when I arrived home, and he was considerably distressed. Not so his sister; she derived a gruesome pleasure in displaying her firmness and self-control and strength of mind in such circumstances, and I loathed her for it.

The first act of business Miss Murdstone performed when the funeral was over, and light was freely admitted into the house, was to give Peggotty two weeks' notice to quit.

"What are you going to do, Peggotty?"

"I'll try to find a position close by so that I can be near to you, Davy, but if I can't then I shall go to my brother's — just till I've had time to look about me for suitable employment in Yarmouth."

But Peggotty's quest round Blunderstone was unsuccessful; the day for her departure dawned all too soon, and Mr Barkis arrived with his faithful horse outside the garden gate.

"Excuse me, miss," said Mr Barkis, after loading up the cart. "I asked this young gentleman 'ere on more than one occasion to tell you that Barkis is willin'. And now I'm tellin' you that Barkis is *still* willin'.'"

If it had not been for the natural redness of Peggotty's complexion, I would have sworn she blushed. "I'm sure I don't know what you're talking about," she replied airily. "Now Davy, I want you to know that you will always be my darlin' boy. I'll come and see you when I can."

"Thank you, Peggotty."

"I'm ready, Mr Barkis," she said firmly, getting into the cart. "And you keep your eyes fixed on that road!"

Peggotty had boldly suggested that since it appeared I was not to return to school, I should go with her for a holiday at Yarmouth. Nothing would have been a greater thrill for me in those trying times.

"The boy will be idle there," retorted Miss Murdstone, "and idleness is the root of all evil; though my brother would appreciate the quiet during his period of suffering more than I can say."

Heaven only knows I was idle enough at Blunderstone. The restraints that used to hold me were now lifted, though I was still not permitted to mix with others of my own age.

I was not ill-treated; I was not beaten or starved. But the wrong that was done to me was unrelenting. Day after day, week after week, month after month, it was as if I just did not exist. I simply fell into a state of neglect.

The only light in this bleak picture came from the visits, every two or three weeks, of dear Peggotty. On one such day, and much to my surprise, she suddenly announced that she was now married.

"That's wonderful!" I cried. "May I ask to whom?"

"To Barkis, of course!" she replied, a little puzzled at my inquiry. "I'll have him as long as he behaves."

We both laughed as she related how, at her brother's boathouse, Barkis had arrived every evening with silly little gifts for her, until she finally agreed to his request; and how they slipped away and were married in a church near Barkis' house, with no-one suspecting any such event until it had been completed.

One evening, after the best part of a year of this weary existence with my guardians, the master of the house announced that he had something of importance to say to me.

"Education is costly, David," he began, his

mean-faced sister standing by his side. "But even if it were not, I am of the firm opinion that it would be no advantage to return you to that school — or to any other. To the young this is a world for action, not for moping in —"

"As you do!" added his sister, looking at me.

"Leave this to me, please, Jane. What is before you is a fight with the world, and the sooner you begin it, the better. I have arranged for you to work at the firm of Murdstone and Grinby, in which I have a small interest, in London. You will earn enough for yourself to live on, with a little more for pocket-money. Your lodgings and washing will be paid for by me."

"You are provided for," observed his sister smugly, "and will be pleased to do your duty."

I have no recollection of whether I was pleased at this turn of events or not, but the very next day I left for London and the morning after that I was put to work in a warehouse cellar down by the river at Blackfriars.

Murdstone and Grinby were wine merchants and my job consisted of examining the returned bottles against the light for flaws and cracks and, if they were not rejected, to wash, rinse, label and re-cork or re-seal them, and put the finished items into cases. For this labour, from eight in the morning until eight at night, I was to be paid the princely sum of six shillings a week.

I was reflecting on the sadness of my plight that first morning when, around midday, there appeared on the steps to the cellar a stoutish, middle-aged person in a red coat, tight brown trousers and black shoes. He boasted an imposing shirt collar and a large top hat.

"Master Copperfield, I presume!" he said, taking off the hat and revealing a head with no more hair upon it than there is upon an egg. "I trust I find you well, sir?"

I said I was, and hoped that he was.

"Yes, quite so. My name is Micawber — Wilkins Micawber. I have been requested by Mr Murdstone to receive you as a lodger, and as I understand that your knowledge of London is not yet extensive, I feel it my duty to present myself in this subterranean workplace at the appropriate time and escort you to my home."

I thanked him heartily for his consideration and told him that I finished at eight o'clock.

He appeared at the appointed time and guided me through the murky streets to his house off the City Road, providing me with such information that I should find my way back in the morning.

Once inside this house — which struck me as like its occupant, shabby but making all the show it could — I was introduced to Mrs Micawber, a thin and faded lady, and to their four small children.

"I never thought that I should find it necessary to take in a lodger," she said when Mr Micawber had disappeared on one of his frequent excursions, "but Mr Micawber being in such dire financial difficulties, all private feelings must be put aside. For all that, Master Copperfield, you are most welcome."

In this house, watching Mr and Mrs Micawber wrestle with their monetary problems and, in vain, to stave off their creditors, I spent most of my precious leisure time. I had little choice, since after paying for my own food there was barely anything left of my wages. When I did decide on a solitary treat, and visited a public house, I was often refused custom because I was so young.

In my forlorn state I became quite attached to the Micawbers and used to walk about, busy with Mrs Micawber's calculations for solving the problems and heavy with the weight of Mr Micawber's debts. On a Saturday night, which was my special treat (I went home early, with six shillings in my pocket), Mrs Micawber would make heart-rending confessions to me. And it would be nothing for Mr Micawber to sob violently at his plight at the start of such an evening, and then be singing his head off with happiness at the end of it. Thus a curious equality of friendship sprung up between us, despite the great disparity in our years.

One summer's day, the very next after Mrs Micawber had confided in me that her husband's difficulties were rapidly coming to a crisis, the said gentleman appeared at my place of work.

"Would you care for some lunch, Master Copperfield?" he asked, handing me a little bundle.

"Thank you, Mr Micawber. Would you like some?"

"Alas, Copperfield, there is no time. The miserable wretch you see before is this very moment the object of much wrath from his creditors. He must flee, Copperfield, flee into the night — or day, as the case may be."

"Do you mean you're leaving London?"

"I am, and I thank you for being a model lodger. Permit me, Copperfield, to leave you two pieces of advice. The first is this: never do tomorrow what you can do today. Procrastination is the thief of time. Collar him! And the second piece of advice is this: annual income twenty pounds, annual expenditure nineteen pounds nineteen and six, result — happiness; annual income twenty pounds, annual expenditure twenty pounds ought and six, result — misery!"

"Is there anything I can do to assist you?"

"Bless you, but no! I trust that we shall meet again. Farewell, my young friend!"

"Goodbye, Mr Micawber, and good luck!"

I had grown so accustomed to the Micawbers, and had been so intimate with them in their distresses, and was so utterly friendless without them, that the prospect of being moved to new and unknown lodgings filled me with panic.

I knew quite well that there could be no escape unless I ordered it myself, and there and then I resolved to run away — to go, by some means or other, down to Dover, to the only relation I had in the world, and tell my story to my great aunt, Miss Betsey Trotwood.

4 A New Life

My journey to Dover was hazardous and long, and only once did I enjoy some respite from walking, when a carrier allowed me to lie on the load in his cart for some six miles or so. Having slept in haystacks and secluded barns, coming within a whisker of danger from other travellers on more than one occasion, I arrived in Dover on the fourth day. It was some hours before I found my aunt's house on the outskirts of the town, by which time I was very nearly on the point of exhaustion.

The first person I saw was a bespectacled gentleman gazing out at me from an upstairs window; but before I had time even to call out to him there appeared another figure through the front door. Immediately I knew her to be Miss Betsey, for she came stalking out of her house exactly as my mother had so often described her stalking into ours at Blunderstone.

"Go away!" she shouted, waving her arms about in the air. "No boys here! Go away!"

"If you please, ma'am — I mean aunt."

"Eh?" she exclaimed, in a tone of amazement I have never heard approached, before or since.

"If you please, aunt, I'm your nephew."

"Oh, Lord!" said my aunt, and she staggered

back to sit down on the garden seat.

"I'm David Copperfield, of Blunderstone, in Suffolk — where you came on the very day I was born, and saw my dear mama. I have been very unhappy since she died. I have been slighted, and taught nothing, and put to work not fit for me. It made me run away to you. I've walked almost all the way here from London, and not slept in a bed since I started the journey —"

Here I broke into a passion of crying, fell down on my knees, and put my aching head on Miss Betsey's lap.

My aunt called up to the gentleman at the window to come down and assist her. "Mr Dick," she said as he approached, "you have heard me mention my nephew, David Copperfield? Now don't pretend not to have a memory, because you and I both know better."

"David Copperfield? *David* Copperfield? Oh yes, to be sure. David. Yes, certainly."

"Well, this is his boy. And he has run away. His sister, Betsey Trotwood, never would have run away, of course, had she been born. But the question is, Mr Dick, what shall I do with him?"

"What shall you do with him?" said Mr Dick, scratching his head. "Why, if I were you, I should — I should — wash him!"

"Of course!" said my aunt. "Oh, you're as sharp as a blade, Mr Dick. That's exactly what we'll do with this boy!"

The bath was a great comfort, and when I was

finished they covered me in a shirt and a pair of trousers belonging to Mr Dick, and put two great shawls around me. What sort of bundle I looked like I don't know, but I was a very hot one, and feeling faint and drowsy, I soon lay down on the sofa and fell fast asleep.

Shortly after I woke we had dinner — never has a meal tasted so sweet — and I told my story in as much detail as I could remember. I was also deeply anxious to know what was to become of me, but I thought it best to avoid such questions so soon after my unexpected appearance.

The next day, at breakfast, I plucked up courage to ask my aunt what she intended to do with me.

"I have written to your stepfather about the subject of your arrival —"

"You're not going to give me up to him?"

"I can't say, I'm sure," replied my aunt. "We shall wait and see."

My spirits sank under these words, and I spent the days waiting for news from Mr Murdstone in a constant state of trepidation. The worry was punctuated, however, by some wonderful hours sharing Mr Dick's passion for flying his kite from the cliffs.

After coming inside from one such sunny afternoon, Miss Betsey asked me what I made of her strange companion.

"I — I think he's very nice," I replied.

"Come now! Your sister Betsey Trotwood would have told what she thought of anyone, straight out. Be as like your sister as you can, and speak out!"

"Is he — is he at all out of his mind, then?"

"Not a morsel! He has been called mad, but if he was I should not have enjoyed the company of his society these past ten years. Mr Dick is a sort of distant relation of mine, but I need not enter into that. If it had not been for my intervention, his brother would have shut him up in an asylum for life. That's all."

This admission increased my growing affection for my aunt — a feeling further enhanced by her attitude on the arrival of Mr and Miss Murdstone the following morning. First, she insisted that I be present throughout the interview; then she gave her visitors a round ticking off for allowing Miss Murdstone's horse to trample on the edge of her lawn; and finally she asked for Mr Dick to come down from his room and introduced him as an old and intimate friend on whose judgment she relied entirely.

Mr Murdstone was the first to broach the subject of their visit. "Miss Trotwood, this unhappy boy who has run away from his friends and his occupation —"

"And whose appearance is quite disgraceful!" interposed his sister.

"Jane, have the goodness not to interrupt when I'm —"

"I'm sorry if his appearance does not agree with you," interrupted my aunt. "Mr Dick was kind enough to relinquish part of his wardrobe to clothe the boy."

"It is not his appearance that concerns me, Miss Trotwood, but his character. This boy has been the cause of much trouble. He has a sullen, rebellious spirit and a violent temper. Both my sister and I have tried to correct his vices, but without success."

"If he had been your own boy, would you have beaten him and sent him off to work in London at such a tender age?" asked my aunt.

"If he had been my brother's own boy," returned Miss Murdstone, striking in, "then his character would, I trust, have been altogether different."

"What have you to say next, eh?" asked my aunt.

"Merely this, Miss Trotwood. I am here to take David back, to dispose of him as I think right. You may have some notion of abetting him in his running away, but I must caution you that if you abet him now, you do so for good and

always. I cannot be trifled with."

"I think I have heard quite enough," said my aunt firmly, rising from her chair. "Mr Dick, what shall I do with this child?"

Mr Dick hesitated for a moment and looked round at me before his face lit up. "Have him measured for a suit of clothes immediately!"

"Mr Dick, give me your hand!" said my aunt triumphantly. "Your common sense is invaluable." She pulled me towards her and said to Mr Murdstone, "You can go when you please. I'll take my chance with the boy. If he is all you say he is, then I can do as much for him as you. But I don't believe a single word of it!"

"Miss Trotwood!" cried Mr Murdstone. "If you were a gentleman —"

"Good day, sir, and goodbye!" said Aunt Betsey. "And good day to you, too, ma'am! Let me see you ride a horse over my green again and as sure as you have a head upon your shoulders, I'll knock your bonnet off and tread upon it!"

The Murdstones left without another word, and my aunt, still with a defiant face, turned to her companion. "You will consider yourself guardian, jointly with me, of this child, Mr Dick?"

"I shall be delighted to be the guardian of such a bright young man! Yes, to be sure — I shall be delighted!"

"Very good," said my aunt with a sigh, "then that's all settled."

I was so happy I clasped both my hands round my aunt's neck and kissed her many times. Then I shook hands with Mr Dick and thanked him over and over again, and he hailed this conclusion to the proceedings with repeated bursts of laughter.

Thus I began my new life and I felt, for many days, like one in a dream. The two clearest things in my mind were that a remoteness had come on the old Blunderstone, which seemed to lie in a distant haze; and that a curtain had fallen on my life at Murdstone and Grinby.

Mr Dick and I soon became the best of friends, and very often went out together to fly his huge kite. Nor did I lose any favour with my aunt, and in the course of a few weeks she took to me so kindly that I was encouraged to feel that I may one day enjoy equal rank in her affections with my fictitous sister, Betsey Trotwood.

"David," she said one evening, when the backgammon board was placed as usual for

herself and Mr Dick, "we must not forget your education. Would you like to go to school at Canterbury?"

I replied that, since it was so near to her, I would like it very much.

"Good. Then would you like to go the day after tomorrow?"

I said I would love to, and so all was made ready.

As we set out, my aunt told me that we were going first to the office of a Mr Wickfield, an old

friend of hers, a lawyer and a steward of the estates of a rich gentleman of the county. When we knocked at the door of his office it was opened by a skeletal-looking young man dressed in legal black.

"Uriah Heep, is Mr Wickfield at home?"

"Yes, ma'am, he is," replied Uriah Heep. "If you'll please to walk in there." And he pointed with his bony hand to another door.

"Well, Miss Trotwood, what a pleasant surprise," said a handsome, well-dressed gentleman. "And what wind blows you here. Not an ill wind, I trust?"

"No, Mr Wickfield. I wish you to draw up adoption papers for my nephew David here, or rather my grand-nephew, and want your advice on a school in Canterbury where he may be thoroughly well taught — and well treated."

"Well, the best school in the district has no room for boarders just now. But I'll tell you what we can do."

"What is that?" inquired my aunt.

"Leave your nephew here, for the present. If it doesn't turn out for the best, there will be time to find another place. We won't be hard about terms, but you shall pay if you will."

"I am very much obliged to you," said my aunt, "and so is he, I see."

"Then I will fetch my little housekeeper," said Mr Wickfield.

He returned with a girl of about my own age. Although her face was quite bright and happy, there was a tranquility about it, and about her — a quiet, calm spirit — that I have never forgotten, and that I shall never forget.

This was his little housekeeper, his daughter Agnes, Mr Wickfield informed us, and she had assured him she would very much like me to board with them.

"Now David," said my aunt, preparing to leave, "never be mean in anything, never be false, and never be cruel; avoid those three vices and I can always be hopeful of you. Be a credit to yourself, to me and to Mr Dick, and may heaven be with you!"

With these words she embraced me and went out of the room, closing the door after her.

Life at Mr Wickfield's house appeared to be very pleasant and peaceful. After dinner we went upstairs to the drawing-room, in one snug corner of which Agnes set a decanter of port wine and glasses for her father. There he sat, taking a good deal of his wine, for two hours, while Agnes played the piano or talked with us. She appeared to be totally devoted to him, and he to her.

The next morning, after breakfast, Mr Wickfield took me to my new school and introduced me to Dr Strong, the headmaster —a gentleman as different from Mr Creakle as it was possible to be. The head-boy, Adams, showed me round and presented me to the masters in a way that would have put me at ease — if anything could, for I was very conscious of the differences in experience and learning between myself and the other boys.

That evening Agnes told me that her mother had died when she was born, and that now, even at her young age, she considered it her duty to stay at home and keep house for her father.

The evening was much the same as the previous one, and on parting to go to bed Mr Wickfield asked me if I thought I should like to stay on with them. I said I should like to very much, and we shook hands on the arrangement.

On the way out to school the following morning I encountered Uriah Heep sweeping the steps outside the house.

"Good morning, Master Copperfield. I trust you'll have a good day at school."

"Thank you, Uriah, and I hope you'll have a good day with your studies in the law."

"Oh, yes, Master Copperfield. When I have the opportunity I am reading *Tidd's Practice*. What a writer Mr Tidd is, Master Copperfield."

"I suppose you are quite a lawyer?"

"Me, Master Copperfield? Oh no, I'm a very 'umble person. I am well aware that I am the 'umblest person going. Let the other be where he may. Likewise my mother is a very 'umble person. We live in an 'umble abode, Master Copperfield, but have much to be thankful for."

"Have you been with Mr Wickfield long?" I asked, mainly to seem agreeable.

"Going on four year, Master Copperfield, since a year after the death of my father."

"Then, when your articled time is over, you'll be a regular lawyer, I suppose. Perhaps one of these days you'll be a partner in Mr Wickfield's business, and it will be 'Wickfield and Heep'."

"Oh, no, Master Copperfield, I am much too 'umble for that!" His mouth widened and the creases in his cheeks deepened and he wriggled about endlessly, shaking his bony head and twisting his hunched body. "Mr Wickfield is a most excellent man, Master Copperfield. If you have known him long, then you know it better than I can inform you."

I replied that I had not known him long, but that he was a friend of my aunt.

"Oh indeed, Master Copperfield. Your aunt is a sweet lady. She has a great admiration for Miss Agnes, I believe?"

I said 'yes', though I knew nothing about it.

"I hope you have, too, Master Copperfield?"

"Everybody must have, Uriah, I would have thought."

"Oh, thank you, Master Copperfield, for that remark. It is so true! 'Umble as I am, I know it to be true. Oh, thank you!"

I made to walk off but Uriah stopped me. "I suppose you will be staying here some time, Master Copperfield?"

I said I believed I would be there as long as I remained at school.

"Oh, indeed! I should think you would come into the business then, Master Copperfield."

I said that I had no views of the kind, and nor had anybody else, but Uriah kept replying to all my assurances until I was forced to be quite off-hand with him in order to get away.

That day I was a little easier at school, and in two weeks or so I was very contented there. I was awkward enough in their games and backward enough in their studies, but practice would improve me in the first, I hoped, and hard work in the second. Fortunately I was to be proved correct in both these judgments.

Every third or fourth week I visited Aunt Betsey in Dover, and on alternate Wednesdays Mr Dick would visit me. He became great friends with Dr Strong and a popular figure at the school, even though he took no active part in any pursuit except kite-flying. Life at the Wickfield home was suitably quiet — and dear Agnes became more of a sister to me than even Aunt Betsey could ever imagine.

5 I Return to London

I am uncertain whether I was glad or sorry when my schooldays drew to an end and the time came for my leaving Dr Strong's. I had been happy there, and I was distinguished in that tiny world; but misty ideas of being a young man of independence were powerful in me.

My aunt and Mr Dick and I had held many serious deliberations on the calling to which I should be devoted — but I had no particular liking, as far as I could discover, for any sphere of activity.

"It had occurred to me, David," said Aunt Betsey one evening, "that a change may be useful in helping you to know your own mind. Suppose you were to go down to the old part of the country again, and see that woman with the strangest of names."

I was more than happy at this suggestion, and wrote to Peggotty to tell her — the latest in a long line of letters I had sent her.

I bade my farewells and took the coach to London, putting up at the Golden Cross hotel. I was making my way from the coffee-room to go to bed when I passed the person who had just come in, and I knew him in a moment. But he didn't seem to know me.

"Steerforth! Won't you speak to me?"

He turned and looked at me, hesitating in his recognition. "My God! It's little Copperfield!"

We ordered some refreshment and exchanged news. He was on his way from the university at Oxford to his mother's home in Highgate, and when I told him of my plans, he invited me to spend a few days there. I enjoyed a glorious, frivolous week in his inspiring company and, after some hesitation on his part, persuaded him to accompany me to Yarmouth.

Over breakfast at the Dolphin Hotel, we agreed that I would go alone to see Peggotty, and that we would rendezvous at the Barkis' house later in the morning.

"Davy, my darlin' boy!" cried Peggotty on my appearance at her door. "How are you? My, look how you've growed! It's so good to see you. Oh, Barkis will be glad."

After she had dried her eyes she led me inside to see her husband, who was laid up in bed with rheumatism.

After a discussion about her husband's health, Peggotty took me through and began preparing dinner, asking all sorts of questions and apologizing for not having replied to as many of my letters as she would have liked. I, in turn, prepared her for the arrival of Steerforth. Like all others before her, she was charmed by his manner and his humour, and we spent a most

enjoyable meal.

On our departure Peggotty was quite insistent that I stay with her during my visit, and my friend concurred. That settled, we made our way through the town and across the sands to the curious boathouse which for two weeks had once been my home. Even as we approached, its three occupants were outside, waving a welcome. "Mas'r Davy!" called out Ham. "It's Mas'r Davy!"

"Hallo, young Davy!" said Mr Peggotty. "It's grand to see you after all this while."

"Hello, Mr Peggotty. Do you remember my friend Steerforth?"

"I do, Davy, I do. He's the sailor and the cricketer."

"Good day, Mr Peggotty, and well met," said Steerforth, shaking him firmly by the hand.

"And this 'ere's Little Em'ly. She ain't my child; I never had one. But I couldn't love her more, you understand?"

"I quite understand," said Steerforth, looking with great interest at Emily. "Well met indeed!"

"But Little Em'ly ain't mine no more. She's engaged to be wed to 'am, these two days past, and will be married when she's of the age!"

"She weren't no higher than you was, Mas'r Davy, when you come to stay," said Ham, softly. "I see her grown up like a flower. I'd lay down my life for her, gentl'men. She's more to me than — than ever I could say. I love her true. There ain't a man in all the land — nor yet sailing on all the sea — that can love his lady more than I love her, though there's many a common man would say better what he meant."

It was moving to see such a sturdy fellow as Ham trembling in the strength of what he felt for the pretty creature who had won his heart.

"I don't know how long I may live, or how soon I may die," said Mr Peggotty, "but if I was capsized in a gale of wind and it was all up with me, I know I could go down quieter for thinkin' that there's a man ashore that's iron-true to my little Em'ly, and that no wrong can touch my darlin' child while it be as that man lives."

We went inside the boathouse and toasted the couple's happiness with all manner of beverages, and passed a wonderful evening there. Steerforth, while setting up no monopoly of the attention, pioneered all the events, and as always took all before him in his stride.

"A most engaging little beauty!" he said as we left to set off across the sands. "Well, it's a quaint place and they're quaint company, and it's quite a new sensation to mix with them!"

"How fortunate we are, too," I replied, "to have arrived to witness their happiness. I never saw people so happy!"

"That's a rather chuckle-headed fellow for the girl, isn't he?"

"Ah, Steerforth. It's well for you to joke about the poor. But I know there is not a joy or sorrow they feel that does not affect you."

"David, I believe you are in earnest, and are good. I only wish we all were!"

He suddenly seemed concerned, almost melancholy. "If anything should ever separate us, David, you must think of me at my best. Come, let us make that bargain! Think of me at my best, if circumstances should ever part us!"

"You have no best to me, Steerforth — and no worst. You are always cherished in my heart."

Steerforth and I were together a good deal during our stay, but he often went sailing with Mr Peggotty, while I spent much time with his sister — as well as making two visits to my parents' graves at Blunderstone.

After nearly three weeks we left, and it seemed that half of Yarmouth had come to see us off. The coach journey on the mail was enlivened by two very different topics, the first of which followed an announcement by Steerforth that he had bought a boat in Yarmouth, that Mr Peggotty would be master of her in his absence — and that, in recognition of Mr Peggotty's passion, he had renamed her 'Little Emily'.

The second discussion, and much more lengthy, was the result of a letter that arrived for me at the hotel that morning. It was from Aunt Betsey, staying in London, inviting me to consider entering the law at the Inns of Court.

Steerforth advised me similarly, and when we came to our journey's end I made my way to Holborn, where I found my aunt up and waiting on her supper.

"Well, David," she began, "what do you think of the plan, eh?"

I said I thought it was an excellent plan, but I was concerned that my entrance into that world would prove very expensive.

"It will cost, to article you, two hundred pounds."

I was astonished at the size of the figure, and begged her to consider whether I was worthy of such an investment.

"David, you have been a credit to me — a pride and a pleasure. I have no other claim upon my means, and you are my adopted child. We need talk of this no more. Now give me a kiss, and we'll make our way to the Inns of Court after breakfast tomorrow."

The next morning we walked to the office of Spenlow and Jorkins, where I was introduced to Mr Spenlow and, following a brief interview, taken into employment as an articled clerk, initially on a month's probation. It was all, indeed, a far cry from the cellars of Murdstone and Grinby, though the institutions were less than a mile apart.

From Spenlow and Jorkins my aunt guided me away to Buckingham Street, in the Adelphi, where we were to view a set of chambers advertized as 'a genteel residence for a young gentleman'. These premises were run by a Mrs Crupp, and proved satisfactory. The following day I moved in, and began life on my own account.

6 Love and Hate

I had been in my chambers two weeks or so when I received a short letter from Agnes, entreating me to visit her in Canterbury, so on the following Saturday I took the Dover Mail.

It was a delight to see her, but we had not been together long before she brought up the reason for her request.

"David, I believe that Uriah is going to enter into partnership with Papa."

"What! Uriah? How could that mean, fawning fellow even be considered for such a promotion? You must protest, Agnes, before it's too late!"

"I'm afraid it is too late, David. He has made himself indispensable to Papa. He has mastered Papa's weaknesses, fostered them, and taken advantage of them until Papa is almost frightened of him."

There was more that she could have said on the matter, but I clearly saw she withheld it from me in order to spare her father.

That evening, at supper, Heep hovered around the table, attending to this and that and ensuring that Mr Wickfield's glass was never empty of wine. After the meal, he said he wished to speak with me.

"What a prophet you have shown yourself, Master Copperfield. You have heard something, I dare say, of a change in my expectations,

Master Copperfield."

"Yes, something."

"I have risen from my 'umble station since first you knew me, Master Copperfield, but I am 'umble still. I hope you will not think the worse of my 'umbleness if I make a little confidence to you, Master Copperfield, will you?"

"If you must."

" 'Umble as I am, Master Copperfield, I love Agnes Wickfield!"

I had the delirious idea of seizing the red-hot

poker from the fire and running him through with it. But I contained myself, and asked him, as casually as I could in the circumstances, whether he had made known his feelings to her.

"Oh no, Master Copperfield! Not to anyone but you! You see, I rest a good deal of hope on her observing how useful I am to her father, and how I keep him straight. She's so much attached to her father, Master Copperfield, that I think she may come, on his account, to be kind to me!"

I fathomed the depth of the rascal's whole scheme, and understood why he laid it bare.

The image of Uriah Heep's ugly figure was still fresh in my mind when, the following week, I was articled to the firm of Spenlow and Jorkins. After we had concluded our business, Mr Spenlow said he would be happy to see me at his house in Norwood the weekend after next, when his daughter would have returned from

completing her education in Paris. We were to drive down in his carriage on the Saturday, and return to London on the Monday morning.

As we went into the house that fateful evening, Mr Spenlow asked a servant where Dora was. "Dora!" I thought. "Dora. What a beautiful name!"

We turned into the breakfast room and I heard a voice say, "Mr Copperfield, my daughter Dora." It was, no doubt, Mr Spenlow's voice, but I didn't know and didn't care. All was over in a moment. I had fulfilled my destiny. I was a captive and a slave. I loved Dora Spenlow to distraction!

The remainder of the evening is lost to me. I don't recall who was there, or what was said, or what we had to eat: only her. I sat next to her. I talked to her. She had the most delightful little voice, the loveliest little laugh, the most fascinating little ways, that ever lost a youth into hopeless slavery. I went to bed, and woke up, in a crisis of feeble infatuation.

I was out in the garden, well before breakfast, when I turned a corner and met her. I tingled from head to foot, and my voice shook as I spoke to her. "You are out early, Miss Spenlow."

"On a Sunday morning, when I don't practise the piano, I must do something. Besides, it's the brightest time of the day. Don't you think so, Mister Copperfield?"

I didn't know what to think, and cannot recall what I replied. I only remember than her dog Jip barked and was mortally jealous of me — and that when she picked him up, and patted him, and laid her chin upon his head, I was mortally jealous of him.

The day passed in a haze of adulation, and I was miserable afterwards that I conveyed nothing of my feelings for her. I was always looking out for another invitation, but as each day drifted by and I received none, I became increasingly disappointed.

I was shocked out of this maudlin state of mind by the sudden appearance of a dear friend. He was waiting for me outside the office late one evening as I left for home.

"Hallo, Davy!"

"Mr Peggotty! What a pleasant surprise! What brings you to London?"

"A grave business, Davy. I've come to find my little Em'ly. She's run off with your friend Steerforth! I've come to search for my neice and

that damned villain, and I'll track 'em down, no matter where they hide."

I will not forget that anguished face and the words that it uttered if I live to be five hundred years. The effect this news wrought on me — and the guilt it inspired — I could not describe.

I took Mr Peggotty to my chambers, and there he told me of the dreadful night of her disappearance, of her note to Ham and himself, begging their forgiveness, of the tears and the wailing and the hate that followed.

"We've had a load of talk, Davy, of what we ought and ought not to do. But I see my course clear. I'm goin' to seek my Em'ly far and wide, and return her to her proper home, if it take me to the end of my nat'ral days! That's my dooty evermore. And if any hurt should come to me — remember Davy, remember that the last words I left her was, 'My unchanged love is with my darlin' child, and I forgive 'er!'"

He suddenly seemed fatigued by the emotion of the telling of his story; I asked him if he had found a room to stay, and he said he was fixed up in a place in Pentonville. Offering my assurance that I would be of help in any form I could, I resolved there and then to ask for leave from my employment and travel to Yarmouth — to do whatever was in my power to comfort Peggotty and poor, deserted Ham.

On the journey I could think of little except my own part in this diabolical affair — of how I had introduced Steerforth to these good people and wrecked so many precious lives.

I found Ham before I reached the boathouse, down by the sea, and even from a distance he looked a forlorn, dejected figure. He turned as I approached, and put on a brave face.

"Hallo, Mas'r Davy. It's good to see you."

"Ham, I'm so sorry that —"

"It ain't no fault of yorn, Mas'r Davy. And you han't no call to be afeered of me. It's done, that's all. The pride and hope of my 'art — her that I'd have died for, would die for now — she's gone!"

I looked at him as he gazed out to sea, and a frightful thought came into my mind. Not that his face was angry; it was not. I recall nothing but an expression of stern determination in it: that if he ever encountered Steerforth, he would surely kill him.

It chanced that while I was in Yarmouth another loss befell this sad community. The state of Mr Barkis' health had deteriorated much in the few weeks since my last visit, so that when I went to see Peggotty at her house she cried and told me he was near his end.

She tried gently to rouse him on my account, but he was senseless. We remained in the room, watching him, for some hours.

"He's a-goin' out with the tide," said Ham, suddenly breaking the silence.

I asked him, in a whisper, what he meant.

"People can't die along the coast, except when the tide's pretty nigh out. They can't be born unless it's pretty high in. He's a-goin' out with the tide."

After some minutes he began to move his head and mumble.

"He's coming to himself," said Peggotty, clutching his hand. "Barkis, my dear!"

"Clara Barkis," he murmured. "No better woman anywheres."

"Look! Here's Master Davy, who brought us together, you remember?"

He half opened is eyes, and I was on the point of asking him if he knew me when he tried to stretch out his arm, and said to me, distinctly, with a pleasant smile: "Barkis is willin'."

And, it being low water, he went out with the tide.

I stayed with Peggotty until after Mr Barkis had made his last journey to Blunderstone, where my old nurse had long since bought a little piece of ground in the churchyard. Despite the trying circumstances, I derived a good deal of satisfaction from being a constant source of comfort to Peggotty and from taking charge of Barkis' will. This turned out to be surprisingly substantial for a man of such modest income (nearly three thousand pounds), and his wife, his brother-in-law and Ham were all to receive significant advantage.

The thought of Dora was a great consolation to me in the subsequent weeks in London. The idea of her was my refuge in disappointment and

distress, and it seemed that the greater the accumulation of trouble in the world, the brighter her star shone above it. Then, one morning, my prayers were answered.

Following a long and not altogether uninteresting discussion about the law in general with Mr Spenlow, he invited me down a week hence for a picnic to celebrate Dora's birthday. I went out of my senses immediately, and think I committed every possible absurdity in preparation for this blessed event. I blush when I remember the cravat I bought; my boots might have been placed in any collection of instruments of torture; I provided, and sent down by coach the night before, a hamper which amounted almost to a declaration of love.

At six in the morning I was in Covent Garden Market, buying a bouquet, and by ten I was trotting down to Norwood on horseback.

Jip barked at me on my arrival, and when I presented my bouquet he bared his teeth at me. Well he might if he knew how much I adored his exquisite mistress!

"Oh, thank you, Mister Copperfield," said Dora. "What lovely flowers!"

I had been practising to say that I had thought them beautiful — before I saw them so near her. But I just could not manage it. She was too bewildering, and I lost all power of language in a dumb ecstasy.

I regained my ability to speak sufficiently to ask her, during the rather crowded picnic, whether she would do me the honour of taking a walk with me, and she consented. Then I hardly knew what I did, I was burning to that extent. But I took Dora's hand and kissed it, and she

smiled, and we all seemed, to my thinking, to go straight up to the seventh heaven.

We did not come down again. We stayed up there all the afternoon and evening. For my part I stayed up there for a week, until the occasion of my next call.

As we walked through the gardens, Dora's shy arm through mine, we found ourselves at the greenhouse. Then — I don't know how I did it — but I did it in a moment! I shut out Jip; I had Dora in my arms; I told her how I loved her, how I should die without her. I told her I idolized and worshipped her. And I embraced her and kissed her upon her lips, and she would not let me draw away.

I suppose we had some notion that this would end in marriage. We must have, because Dora stipulated that we were never to be married without her father's consent. We were to keep our secret from Mr Spenlow, but I'm sure the idea never entered my head, then, that there was anything dishonourable in that understanding.

What a happy, foolish time it was that followed! Of all the times of mine, there is none that I can smile at half so much, and think of half so tenderly.

7 Two Dreams Come True

I was still in this blissful state some weeks later when I saw before me in the street a figure who, though unmistakably not from another world, may just as well have been for the advancement in my fortunes since last I had seen him.

"Mr Micawber! Mr Micawber!"

At first he did not know me in the least, though he stood face to face with me. Then he examined my features with more attention, fell back, and cried: "Is it possible? Do I again have the pleasure of beholding Copperfield, the companion of my youth?"

"You do, Mr Micawber. Indeed you do! And how are you — and Mrs Micawber?"

"You find us, Copperfield, established on an unassuming scale. But you are aware that I have, in my career, surmounted difficulties and conquered obstacles. You are no stranger to the fact that there have been periods of my life when it has been requisite that I should fall back, before making what I trust I shall not be accused of presumption in terming — a spring. The present is one of those momentous stages in the life of man. You find me, Copperfield, fallen back, for a spring, and I have every reason to believe that a vigorous leap will shortly be the result."

"I'm sure you will spring like a tiger, Mr Micawber. In the meantime, could I invite you and your good wife to dine with me in my chambers tomorrow evening at eight o'clock?"

"Young Copperfield in chambers! Oh, Time, you are a thief and a rogue! We should be delighted, my friend, and you may depend upon it that we shall be hungry!"

At the appointed time my guests arrived, and both were delighted with my residence.

"My dear Copperfield, this is luxurious. It is a way of life which reminds me of the period when I was myself in a state of celibacy, and Mrs Micawber had not yet been solicited to plight her faith at the altar."

"He means solicited by him, Mr Copperfield," said Mrs Micawber. "He cannot answer for others."

"Now tell me, Copperfield. With the example of such a tested union as ours before you, have you any thoughts on the twin peaks of human existence — namely love and marriage — to occupy your mind at present?"

"I have indeed, Mr Micawber," I replied, blushing just a little, and I informed them of my love for Dora.

After celebration of this state of affairs with several toasts, the conversation took a more practical turn, with Mrs Micawber extolling the professional abilities, as yet unappreciated, of her dear husband.

We were discussing how these talents could best be brought to the notice of society when there was a knock on the outer door to my rooms. I opened it to be greeted by the astonishing spectacle of my aunt and Mr Dick — she sitting upon a large trunk and he clutching his beloved kite!

"Aunt Betsey! Mr Dick!"

"David!" said my aunt, brusquely. "Have you become firm and self-reliant?"

"I — I hope so, aunt."

"Then why, my dear boy, why do you think I prefer to sit upon this property of mine tonight?"

I shook my head, unable even to guess.

"Because, David, it's all I have. Because I'm ruined, my dear!"

I was still recovering from the shock of this news when there was a voice at my shoulder.

"Fear not, my dear lady!" said Mr Micawber boldly. "I have no scruple in saying that I am a man who has, for some years, contended against the pressures of monetary difficulties. I have been to the land of penury, but I have returned. Madam, all is not lost!"

My aunt seemed not in the least put out by this intrusion, and took it in the spirit in which it had been made. "Your eloquent friend is right, David. We must meet our reverses boldly, and not suffer them to frighten us. We must learn to act the play out. We must live misfortune down!"

At this point Mr Dick clapped his hands several times in appreciation.

I invited my unexpected visitors inside and introduced them to the Micawbers, who, after expressing the appropriate sentiments, left us to our own devices.

My aunt explained that she had become dissatisfied with her financial advisor and had taken it upon herself to make her own investments, through Mr Wickfield's firm. All had ended in failure, she had been informed, and the finish was very sudden. Apart from the belongings still on the landing, all she had in the world was her cottage.

I ventured that I must do something to help her in her distress.

"Go for a soldier, do you mean?" returned my aunt. "Or go to sea? I won't hear of it. We're not going to have any knockings on the head in this family, sir, if you please!"

It was getting late, and we left these grand concerns to talk of more immediate problems. It was decided that I take Mr Dick round to a boarding-house in Hungerford Market, while Aunt Betsey was to stay with me. She was to have my room, and I was to bed down in the sitting-room by the fire, to keep guard over her.

I decided to pay no heed to my aunt's advice — heaven knows she had been generous enough to me — and the next morning I asked Mr Spenlow if I might cancel my articles with his firm and reclaim her investment. He maintained that he himself would have no objection — despite the awkward precedent it would set — but was convinced that his partner, Mr Jorkins, would be quite immovable on such a subject.

That evening I found a letter from Agnes waiting for me in my chambers, the contents of which I found very disturbing. Uriah Heep was now a partner, and he and his dreadful mother had moved into the Wickfield house. I replied by

return to say that I would be down to Canterbury at the very next opportunity.

This mission was delayed by the sudden death of Dora's father, who collapsed in his carriage one evening on the way home to Norwood. The business thus needed extra attention for some weeks — indeed it soon began to fall off quite badly — but my main concern was for my dear sweetheart.

I had now a morbid jealousy of death, that it would keep her from me; and so in a way it did, since she now fell under the protection of two aunts who lived together in Putney. Neither had seen their neice since her christening, but they now assumed responsibility for her welfare and spirited her away.

It was some while until, prompted by the advice of Agnes, I grew sufficiently bold to tell them of our situation; and eventually, after a long and almost paralyzing wait, Dora and myself were officially engaged to be married.

The following week I set off for Canterbury, calling first at Dover to check on the tenants of Aunt Betsey's cottage. Imagine my surprise when, on entering the office now marked 'Wickfield and Heep', I should see none other than Mr Micawber plying his pen at Uriah's old desk! After our customary exchanges, he explained that he had raised the funds necessary to advertize his talents — the great spring to which he had alluded in London — and that one Uriah Heep had engaged him as 'a confidential clerk'.

"And how do you like the law, Mr Micawber?" I asked.

"My dear Copperfield, to a man possessed of the higher imaginative powers, the objection to legal studies is the amount of detail they involve.

Even in our professional correspondence, the mind is not at liberty to soar to any exalted form of expression. Still, it is a great pursuit!"

He then informed me that he had become the tenant of Uriah Heep's former house, and that he and Mrs Micawber were comfortable. But I detected a change in him, as if his duties did not suit him.

On my way to see Agnes I was intercepted by Uriah Heep, who invited — or rather badgered — me into his office. He asked me about my feelings towards Agnes; indeed he was so insistent that I found myself declaring my brotherly love for her, and confessing that I was recently engaged to Dora.

This seemed to please him enormously and at dinner, flushed with new confidence, he enticed Mr Wickfield into a series of toasts. Finally, when Agnes had left us, he raised his glass and in a gesture of triumph said, "Gentlemen, I give you Agnes Wickfield, the divinest of her sex! To be her father is a proud distinction, but to be her 'usband —"

"No! No!" cried Mr Wickfield, his face distorted with impotent rage. "Look at my torturer! Before him I have, step by step, abandoned name and reputation, house and home! Oh, see the millstone he is about my neck!"

"You had better stop him, Copperfield, if you can," sneered Uriah, pointing. "He'll say something presently he'll be sorry to have said afterwards, and you'll be sorry to 'ave 'eard!"

I did not even have to consider stopping him, because at that moment the door opened and Agnes came in. She helped her distraught father out of his chair and up to the drawing-room.

The next morning, over breakfast, I pleaded with Agnes not to marry Heep from a mistaken sense of duty; but despite my protestations, she would not give me that promise.

Shortly after this unhappy episode, Dora and I were married. Few attended the wedding and when the guests had left we settled down to married life. I must confess that Dora found domestic chores uncongenial; indeed, despite the advice and help first of Peggotty and then Aunt Betsey, she never ever began to master the art of managing the household.

Life too changed for me. What had once been just a hobby — writing stories for magazines — soon became a full-time occupation and by the end of the year I left the employment of Spenlow and Jorkins to devote myself to my first novel.

It was on the penultimate day of my stay at Spenlow and Jorkins that I unexpectedly met Mr Peggotty. It was a cold night, so I invited him to a tavern so that we could talk.

This tireless wanderer had been away for some months, searching alone for his beloved Emily and her lover. He had been to France, to Italy, to Switzerland, nearly always travelling on foot, and had come close to finding them on more than one occasion. But the trail had disappeared, and now he had come back to London, via Yarmouth.

Whilst in London he had discovered from a girl named Martha, who was also from Yarmouth, the whereabouts of his young neice.

"Martha's to meet me on the north side of Westminster Bridge tomorrow night, at ten," said Mr Peggotty, "and take me to my darlin' child. I'd be more than happy if you'd come with me, Davy, if you can!"

We met Martha at the appointed time. In complete silence she led us along the murky waterfront. After some time, she darted into a dark entrance and up some stairs to the second floor of an old house. Still not a word was spoken. We opened the door and stood inside, waiting. A thin, frightened figure appeared from behind a screen, and peered at us for a moment.

"Uncle!"

A fearful cry followed the word; then, with a start, Emily fell insensible, into the arms of Mr Peggotty. He gazed for a few seconds into her face, then kissed her gently.

"Davy," he said quietly, looking up at me. "I thank my 'eavenly father as my dream's come true! I thank him hearty for guidin' me, in his own strange ways, to my darlin' child!"

With those words he took her up in his arms and carried her, motionless and still unconscious, down the broken stairs and out into the dark night.

The next day Mr Peggotty came round to see

me. "All night long," he began, the tears welling in his eyes, "her arms have been about my neck, and we knows full well that we can trust each other ever more. I want to thankee, Davy, for coming last night, and for being my friend."

He told me that at first Emily and Steerforth had indeed ventured all over Europe; but in Naples — he growing restless and she becoming melancholy — he had abandoned her. She had worked her own passage home, finally encountering her old friend Martha on the streets of London.

"And what of the future, Mr Peggotty?"

"I've made up my mind, Davy, and told little Em'ly. There's mighty countries, far from here, and our future lies over the sea. No-one can't reproach my darlin' in Australia. We sail in six weeks. But there's one thing more, Davy. I can't take Em'ly to Yarmouth and I can't leave her here, neither; so I've writ letters to Clara and Ham, setting everything down. Could you take them for me, Davy, and take my farewell leave of Yarmouth for me?"

As on my previous visit, it was easy to come Ham's way, and I told him all that had happened in London.

"When you see her, Mas'r Davy," said Ham, "there's somethin' I could wish said. It ain't that I forgive her — it ain't that so much. 'Tis more that I beg *her* to forgive *me*, for havin' pressed my

affections on her. Odd times I think that if I hadn't had her promise to marry me, she might have told me what was struggling in her mind, and I might have saved her."

"Is there anything more?" I asked.

"Yes, Mas'r Davy. The last you see of him — the very last — will you give him the lovingest duty and thanks of the orphan, as he was ever more than a father to?"

I promised faithfully to convey both these messages, and set off to see Peggotty.

8 Gains and Losses

Soon after my return from Yarmouth there arrived a letter from Mr Micawber, in which he implored Aunt Betsey, Mr Dick and myself to be at his office at half-past nine the next day but one, about a matter of the utmost importance. He claimed that our presence was essential to his design, and that it was to our advantage to attend.

I was somewhat uneasy about leaving Dora to obey this strange call, since she was in some distress with a mild fever, but she insisted that both my aunt and myself travel to Canterbury.

We were greeted at the door of Wickfield and Heep by Mr Micawber, who now seemed more like his old self once more.

"Mr Micawber," said Aunt Betsey, "perhaps you would be so good as to tell us why you have called us here today?"

"To expose villainy and corruption, my dear lady," replied Mr Micawber, pointing to the skies, "and to restore your fortunes. Two noble causes, I think you will agree! Now, please step this way."

He led us in and, without knocking, opened the door to Uriah's office. The occupant rose from his chair as Mr Micawber ushered us in. Our visit astonished him, evidently — not the least, I dare say, because it astonished ourselves — but in a moment he had recovered and was as fawning as ever.

"Well, well, this is indeed an unexpected pleasure, I'm sure. Things have changed since I was an 'umble clerk in this office, Miss Trotwood, 'aven't they? But I 'aven't changed, Miss Trotwood."

"No," returned my aunt, coldly. "I think you have been pretty constant to the promise of your youth, if that's any satisfaction to you."

"Oh thank you, Miss Trotwood," replied Uriah, writhing in his ungainly manner and turning to his clerk. "Don't wait, Micawber."

Mr Micawber, with his hand upon a ruler in his breast pocket, stood erect before the door.

"What are you waiting for, Micawber? Go along, I'll talk to you presently."

"If there is a scoundrel on this earth with whom I have already talked too much," said Mr Micawber, leaning slightly forward, "that scoundrel's name is — *Heep!*"

Uriah fell back, as if he had been struck or stung. "Oho, this is a conspiracy! You have met here by appointment. You are playing games with my clerk, Copperfield, are you? Well take care, for I'll counterplot you!"

"Mr Micawber," I said grandly, "you may deal with this fellow as he deserves."

Mr Micawber produced from his pocket a document folded in the form of a letter, and began to read: "In an accumulation of want, despair, shame and madness, I entered the office of the firm called Wickfield and Heep, but in reality wielded by Heep alone. Heep, and only Heep, is the mainspring of that machine, and Heep, and only Heep, is the forger and the cheat!"

"The devil take you, Micawber!" cried Uriah, taking a grab at the letter and receiving a crack with the ruler on his knuckles. "I'll be even with you!"

"Approach me again, you — you — Heep of infamy, and if your head is human, I'll break it. Come on, come on!"

I think I never saw anything more ridiculous — I was aware of it, even at the time — than Mr Micawber's gestures against his cringing enemy. When I had cooled him down, he continued with his letter.

"Soon after entering the employment of Wickfield and Heep I found the salary of twenty-two shillings and sixpence insufficient to alleviate the poverty of my family. I than sank into a state of indebtedness to the snake Heep in the form of IOUs. In return for securing these I was called upon to forge the signature of Mr Wickfield in the pursuit of defrauding both himself and his clients, including Miss Trotwood."

Mr Micawber then read out a long list of specific charges against Heep and put down the letter. "All this I undertake to show," he concluded with a flourish, "and I have the necessary documentation in my possession!"

Suddenly Uriah took out a large key and opened the safe. It was empty.

"All the books are in good hands!" said Mr Micawber.

"So, Heep," said my aunt after a pause, "it is

you who have ruined me!"

"Fear not, dear lady!" cried Mr Micawber. "All shall be returned to you!"

I suggested that Heep be confined to his room until matters were completed, but he agreed only after my aunt threatened to fetch two officers of the law. She then turned her attention to the delicate question of Mr Micawber's future.

"Mr Micawber, I wonder if you have ever turned your thoughts to emigration? It seems to me that Australia would be a legitimate sphere of action for your talents. And I'm sure my present good fortune could suffer a substantial loan."

"Madam, I hear the call of the wild, and the call is Australia!"

We returned home in understandably high spirits. But the euphoria was short-lived, for Dora was now desperately ill, and in a matter of days it became obvious to all that she would not recover. I hardly left her side, but there was nothing I could do. Impotently, I watched her slip away from me. Weak as she was, she begged me to send for Agnes. The two saw each other alone and what was said was not revealed to me until much later. But when Agnes came back downstairs, it was, I knew, all over — I had lost my darling for ever.

Gradually, as I began to recover from the depths of my misery, it was proposed that I go abroad. But it was to Yarmouth that I turned.

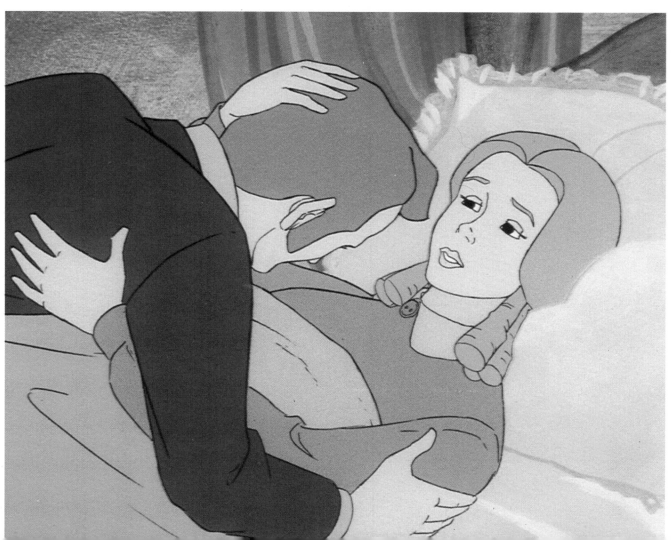

The day after Dora's funeral, and in response to the message I conveyed from Ham to Emily, Mr Peggotty showed me a note from Emily to Ham. She had requested that I read it — it was the most touching of communications — and take

charge of it, in case of reply. Under the circumstances I was even more glad than usual to be of service and set off on the coach down the road I had travelled in so many different moods and in so many varied causes.

Yet never had I seen a sky like this one — on this road or indeed anywhere. There had been a strong wind all day, but as afternoon passed into evening it rose higher and higher, and sweeping gusts of rain came up like showers of steel.

I put up at the Dolphin Hotel, then went in search of Ham along the windswept shore; but he was not at his house, nor the yard where he worked. I began to feel an uneasiness about his not being there when I saw a great commotion down by the shore — and then, through the waves and the foam, the sight of a ship pitching and rolling in the heaving seas.

In all the shouting and the noise I made out that she was a schooner from Spain or Portugal, loaded with fruit and wine, and that some crew were still thought to be on board. The lifeboat had been manned an hour since but could make no contact, and as no man had attempted to make off from the boat with a rope and try to establish communication with the shore, there was nothing more to be done.

Then the crowd parted and Ham strode forward, a rope over his shoulder. I ran to him, imploring him not to go, then pleading with his fellow men not to let him. But I might as well have entreated the wind.

"If my time is come, Mas'r Davy, 'tis come," he said, grasping me with both hands. "If it ain't, I'll bide it. Lord above bless you, and bless all! Mates, make me ready. I'm a-going off!"

Ham watched the sea until there was a great retiring wave; then, with a backward glance at those who held the rope made fast round his body, he dashed in after it, and in a moment was buffeting with the water; rising with the hills, falling with the valleys, lost beneath the foam; then drawn again to land. They hauled it hastily.

He was hurt. I saw blood on his face, but he took no thought of it. He seemed to give them directions for leaving him more free, and was then gone as before.

Now he made for the wreck, striving hard and valiantly. The distance was nothing, but the power of the sea and wind made the strife deadly. At length he reached the wreck. He had, somehow, managed to pull himself aboard,

when a vast hillside of water moving on shoreward from beyond the ship engulfed it, and it was gone.

They drew him to my very feet — insensible — dead. Every means of restoration were tried, but all in vain. He had been beaten to death by the great wave, and his generous heart was stilled for ever.

I knelt down beside him, the note from Emily gripped in my hand. I looked up to see another body being carried up the beach. They laid the poor wretch down next to Ham, his head resting on his arm.

I thought at first sight that my mind was confused by tragedy and long exposure to the fierce wind and great roar of the storm; but I was not mistaken. On that part of the beach where I had looked for shells with Emily, on that part of it where some lighter fragments of the old boathouse, blown down by the storm, had been scattered by the wind, among the ruins of the home he had wronged — I saw Steerforth lie with his head upon his arm, as I had so often seen him lie at school.

The effect these two grievous losses had on me — and so soon after the angel of death had taken Dora — I cannot begin to describe. I resolved to adopt my initial idea and go abroad to write, and following the safe departure of the emigrants from Gravesend — the Micawber family, Mr Peggotty, Emily and Martha — I travelled slowly to Switzerland, leaving behind all those who

were dear to me.

The solitude seemed to increase the power of my pen, and in a short time I became not only a successful novelist but also quite a famous one.

The great joy in my lonely life were the letters of Agnes, and as the time passed and my third summer abroad approached, I began to realize that my love for her — a very different love from

that I had felt for Dora — was far more than that of a brother, and always had been.

And so I returned to Dover, and the very next day rode to Canterbury. I had nurtured fears about Agnes being committed to another, about her not seeing me in the same light as I now saw her. But all these were ill-founded. She was as gentle and charming as ever; and when I confessed that I felt for her more than a mere brother, she said that she had to confess to me that she had always felt more than a sister should to me. We spoke no more words, but sealed our new love with a kiss.

How happy we were! How right it all seemed! We were soon married, and as we rode away, through the gates of Canterbury, Agnes turned to me and said: "Dearest husband! Now that I may call you that, I have one thing more to tell you. On the night Dora died, she made a last request to me, and left me a last charge."

"And what was it, my darling?"

"That only I would occupy this vacant place."

And Agnes laid her head upon my breast, and wept; and I wept with her, though we were so very happy.

Epilogue

There is yet one incident which I must relate to complete my record.

I had advanced in fame and fortune and been married ten wonderful years. Agnes and I were sitting by the fire in our London home, and three of our children were playing in the room, when I was told that a stranger wished to see me.

It was no stranger: it was none other than Mr Peggotty. An old man now, but in a ruddy, hearty, strong old age. When our first emotion was over, and he sat before the fire with the children on his knees, he told us of our friends' fortunes in Australia.

They had all fared well, by all accounts, in the change from the sea to the land. Emily was with him, at home, always the first to do someone a kindness, and constantly turning down offers of marriage; Martha, however, had married in their second year, to a farm labourer who lived four hundred miles off in the bush land.

Mr Micawber and his family had worked as hard as Mr Peggotty had seen anyone work, and he had at last achieved the position of respect he desired. The visitor produced a copy of the local paper as illustration, and indeed Mr Micawber's influence was everywhere in it, not least in the report of a public dinner 'in honour of our distinguished townsman and magistrate'. There was also a letter in the paper from the said gentleman and addressed to *David Copperfield, Esq., the eminent author*, in which he sent the greetings of himself and his community.

Before Mr Peggotty left for Australia a month later he went with me to Yarmouth, to see a tablet I had put up in the churchyard to the memory of Ham. While I was copying the plain inscription for him, at his request, I saw him stoop and gather a tuft of grass from the grave.

"For Em'ly," he said, as he put it in his breast. "I promised, Davy."

We also journeyed to Dover, to see his sister — wearing spectacles now and a good deal thinner, but still my old nurse, and still a housekeeper. And Aunt Betsey, an old woman of four-score years and more but upright yet, and a steady walker of six miles at a stretch in winter weather. Her old disappointment is set right now, for she is godmother to a real living Betsey Trotwood; and Dora (the next in order) says she spoils her. And Mr Dick, making giant kites among my sons, and taking me aside to whisper in my ear that "your aunt's the most extraordinary woman in the world, sir!"

And what of those far from dear to me? Uriah Heep made off with his mother to London, not without funds, but is at present residing in a Middlesex prison after convictions for fraud, forgery and conspiracy. Power, not money, was always his ambition.

Of the Murdstones I know only because the doctor who delivered this writer into the world has moved to the village where they now reside near Bury St Edmunds. He married yet another lively young woman and now he and his sister have also destroyed her with their gloom and austerity. They go about with her, it is said, more like her keepers than her husband and sister-in-law. I can all too easily believe it to be the sorry truth.

But one face, shining on me like a heavenly light by which I shall see all other objects, is above all. I turn my head and see it, in its beautiful serenity, beside me. O, Agnes, so may thy face be by me when I close my life.